T is for Tutu
A Ballet Alphabet

Written by Sonia Rodriguez & Kurt Browning
and Illustrated by Wilson Ong

For our two favorite little dancers, Gabriel and Dillon,
whose laughter fills our lives with joy.
—Sonia and Kurt

To Tess, may your childhood be filled with music, dance, and joy.
—Wilson

Text Copyright © 2011 Sonia Rodriguez & Kurt Browning
Illustration Copyright © 2011 Wilson Ong

Sleeping Bear Press™
315 E. Eisenhower Parkway, Ste. 200
Ann Arbor, MI 48108
www.sleepingbearpress.com

Sleeping Bear Press is an imprint of Gale, a part of Cengage Learning.

First Edition

10 9 8 7 6 5 4 3 2 1

Printed by China Translation & Printing Services Limited,
Guangdong Province, China. 1st printing. 05/2011

Library of Congress Cataloging-in-Publication Data

Rodriguez, Sonia.
T is for tutu : a ballet alphabet / written by Sonia Rodriguez & Kurt Browning;
Illustrated by Wilson Ong.
p. cm.
ISBN 978-1-58536-312-4
1. Ballet—Juvenile literature. 2. Alphabet books—Juvenile literature.
I. Browning, Kurt. II. Ong, Wilson, ill. III. Title.
GV1787.5.R63 2011
792.8—dc22
2010030385

A a

A is for Anybody—
anybody can dance.
All you have to do
is give yourself a chance.

Follow the rhythm,
move to the beat,
and you're already dancing.
Isn't that neat?

The first thing you need to know about dancing is that you really don't need to know anything about dancing! There are no rules when you're dancing for fun. You don't need to go to school to learn to skip down the street, and you don't need lessons to move to the beat. Dance is something to enjoy whether you are young or old, girl or boy.

The beginning of ballet can be traced all the way back to the fifteenth century and the Italian courts. Wealthy nobles gave grand banquets and balls—large dances where participants wore formal clothing—to impress their guests.

But it is Louis XIV of France who takes credit for what we today call professional ballet. Until then, ballet was only supported by and performed for the nobility, making it a privilege. In 1661 Louis decided to set up an academy, The Académie Royale de Musique, for the training of dancers, giving ballet a professional look. This took ballet to the stage and offered the world the first professional ballet school and company. For a hundred years the development of professional ballet would remain in Paris, where it began, but today ballet is performed all around the world—an art form shared and loved by many.

B is for Ballet
where little girls wear
pretty pink tutus
and flowers in their hair.

The boys in ballet
learn to jump high.
And as they grow strong
they just seem to fly.

Cc

An essential part of a developing dancer is the ballet class. Beginners may start with a class once or twice a week and gradually add more days of training. A dancer who hopes to become a professional will most likely take classes at least five days a week. The level of difficulty of each class will vary depending on the dancer's age and ability, but the structure of classes remains the same.

A class is composed of two very distinct parts, the barre and the center. The barre consists of a series of exercises that dancers perform holding onto a barre, a stationary handrail usually made of wood. At the barre, a dancer focuses on finding her center of balance and works on proper body alignment.

The center is the second part of the class. Its name comes from the fact that a dancer is no longer assisted by the barre but performs the exercises in the middle of the studio.

These routines apply what the dancer has already accomplished at the barre but now the focus is on movement, turns, and jumps.

C is for the Class
    you could take every day.
You work on your technique
    and improve in every way.

You will start at the barre
    where movements are not too fast.
Then you'll move to the center
    where you'll spin and jump at last.

The universal language of ballet is French, and pas de deux means "step for two" in French. With assistance from a boy dancer, the girl is able to jump higher and position her body in ways she cannot do on her own unless he is there to stabilize her. With his help, her jumps become much higher, and she can execute many more turns in a row. Together they can perform explosive and exciting lifts to impress the audience. Both dancers need strength and precision, and both dancers have important roles during a pas de deux.

Any dance choreographed for two, a girl and a boy or two boys or two girls, is considered a pas de deux. In classical ballet a grand pas de deux is choreographed for a male and a female dancer, and consists of three distinct parts: adagio (both dancers perform together); variation (each dancer performs a solo dance); and coda (the finale that brings the pas de deux to a conclusion).

D is for a dance
that is made for two.
Do you know what it's called?
I just gave you a clue.

It has a French name.
Do you want to guess?
If you said "pas de Deux"
then the answer is yes.

Dd

Dance exams are a way to test students' abilities and gauge their improvement. Exam day is exciting, and each student wants to do his or her best! Together, class instructors and dance students have been preparing routines for exam day.

Each dance student receives a number to pin on his or her leotard. This number identifies the dancer and ensures that exam results do not get mixed up. The examiner then asks each dancer to take his or her place at the barre and later at the center to perform.

Students are tested differently all around the world. In most countries in Europe, exams are government regulated and carried out at national conservatories of dance. In North America, some schools do their own evaluations. There are also examination associations that provide testing guidelines, and an examiner is available for smaller dance schools.

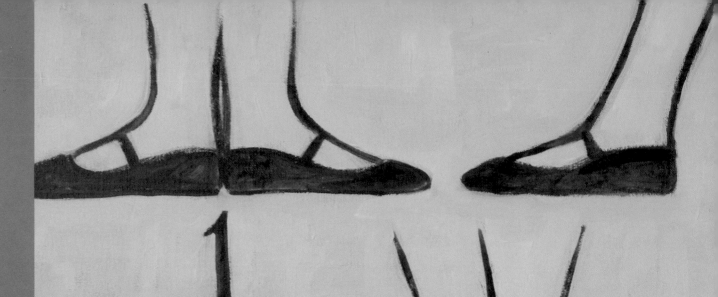

E is for the dance Exams,
a right that you have earned.
They're your chance to show everyone
all that you have learned.

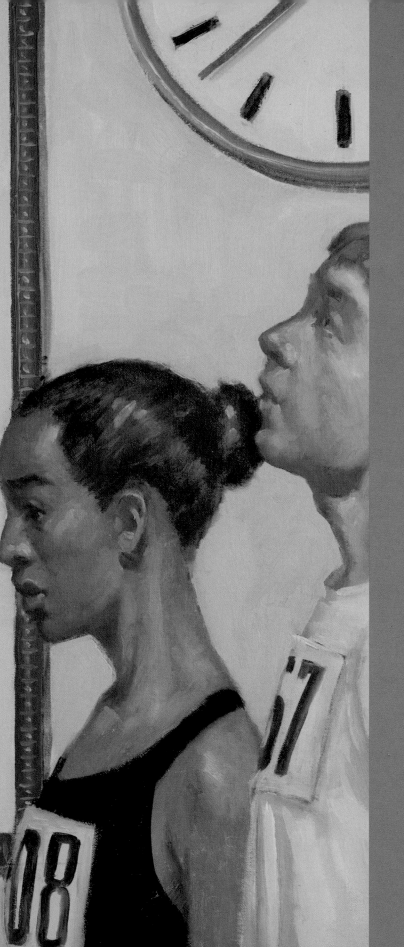

2

$F$is for the Five Positions that ballet dancers do. Look at the feet in the picture— now you know them, too.

5

Ballet is based on five classic positions of the feet. The positions were created by Pierre Beauchamp around 1700 and for more than 300 years they have been the foundation for ballet. These five positions form a base for the dancer to stand as well as to move in any direction. The positions are based on turnout, which is the ability of the dancer to literally "turn out" his or her hips and knees, but much further than a person would in everyday movements. Practice and stretching allow a dancer to create beautiful positions and lines with the body that would otherwise be impossible.

Giselle is one of the finest ballets from the Romantic Era (roughly 1780 to 1850). A ballet in two acts, it was first produced in Paris in 1841 with Carlotta Grisi in the title role and Lucien Petipa as the Count Albrecht. Like all the romantic ballets, *Giselle* offers two worlds, one of reality and one of fantasy. In the first act, Giselle is a peasant girl who falls in love with a count in disguise. When his real identity is revealed, and she learns that he is already promised to another woman, she dies of a broken heart. In the second act Count Albrecht is captured by the Wilis, the spirits of young women who loved to dance and died before their wedding day. Albrecht is ordered to dance to his death but the spirit of Giselle appears, and her love for him saves his life.

The role of Giselle demands great technique and acting ability but the greatest challenge is the dual role presented to the ballerina. Some feel more comfortable performing as the peasant girl, others more as the spirit. Mastering both styles is a great challenge, and ballerinas from around the world aspire to dance the part of Giselle.

G is for *Giselle,*
a ballet story of
an innocent young maiden
and her tragic love.

Dance has so many tales,
and on the stage they're told.
Some of them are new
but most are very old.

H is for the History of dance,
which takes us back in time,
back as far as primitive man
whose dance was based on mime.

It is impossible to say exactly when dance truly began. The appearance of dance patterns in the movements of animals and birds shows that dance probably originated with them. Primitive man may have danced originally out of impulse or amusement, or like the birds, in courtship. Today, people dance mainly for enjoyment, but for primitive man, dancing served different purposes; dance gave humans a way to communicate with each other before language skills were developed.

Mime uses gestures to share stories, demonstrate needs, and to express thoughts and feelings. By observing tribal dances performed today, we can guess that following the Stone Age, humans developed dances for every important occasion: marriage, birth, death, and war, and to make contact with their gods. There were also ritual dances for any occasion that required magic or superior powers.

As with any other physical activity, dancing poses some risk of injury. A dancer dreads any injury because it could mean that he or she must take time away from training or performing. In some cases, it may be necessary for a doctor to assess an injury and perhaps recommend physical therapy and time off from dancing. As a dancer grows and the physical demands of training increase, it is very important to give the body the attention it needs to avoid injuries.

Nutrition plays an important role in allowing a dancer's body to keep up with the physical demands. Healthy eating also helps to repair and build muscle, bone, and tissue.

I is an Injury
that could happen to you.
But you will recover
once you know what to do.

I is for Investing
in rest and proper care,
so you'll continue dancing
like the injury was never there.

I i

J j

J is for Joyous Jumps
like the grand jeté.
They all start and end
with a demi plié.

The demi plié, or bending of the knees with heels on the ground, is an essential part of any jump. It allows for elevation in the takeoff and absorbs the impact during landing. Jumps are usually steps used to highlight the male dancer. A very popular jump is the grand jeté, in which the dancer leaps forward splitting legs, performing an aerial split. This jump is commonly performed in sequence in a circular pattern called *manège*.

There was a time when dance was dominated by men. Dance was considered a necessary art for physical development, an important skill for any nobleman, and was even used in the training of soldiers. The role of the male dancer was very strong until the Romantic Era and the invention of pointe shoes. This brought the ballerina into the spotlight, and the role of the male dancer became secondary. Only in Eastern Europe, Russia, and Denmark did male dancing continue to develop. In North America the role of the male dancer was influenced by other types of dance. Spanish dancing, considered one of the most masculine dances, and Fred Astaire's jazz style and personality, had a big impact on how the public regarded men as dancers.

There have been many great male ballet dancers throughout history but the one who really changed the image of the male dancer was Rudolf Nureyev. Originally from Leningrad in the Soviet Union, Nureyev defected to the west in the early 1960s and immediately became a superstar, gaining enormous respect and popularity. He made the role of the male ballet dancer as important as the ballerina's role.

K is for King—
a boy's role to play.
With a crown and his sword
he often saves the day.

There are also mean wizards
and handsome princes, too.
In so many ballet stories
there's a lot that boys can do.

L l

From young students to professional dancers, the leotard, worn with tights, is the practice clothing of choice. Made to fit like a second skin, the leotard allows the dancer a full range of movement and offers the teacher an unobstructed view of the lines of the body, making it easier to correct any flaws that the dancer may have in his or her technique. The material is usually a combination of spandex and cotton, with a wide selection of designs and colors to choose from.

Many dance schools choose a particular leotard design and color in order to create uniformity in the class. In this sense the leotard becomes the dancer's uniform. It is important to realize that the leotard is not only worn by dancers in the studio—but that it is also used as a costume by modern dancers and by ballet dancers in many contemporary works.

L is for the Leotard
that shows the dancer's form.
When dancers are rehearsing,
it becomes a uniform.

The relationship between music and dancing is unique. Each element can exist without the other, but when performed in perfect harmony, they become a single unit. Usually a piece of music is chosen first, and the dancing is choreographed later. How the dance is choreographed—made up or planned—has a lot to do with the rhythm and tempo of the music.

When planning a new ballet, a choreographer can either use music that has already been written or ask a person called a composer to write new music. Sometimes ballet music is played by just a few musicians or by a full symphony orchestra. An orchestra usually includes musicians playing string, woodwind, or brass instruments.

A fun way to realize how music affects dance is to listen to different kinds of music and let your body move to the various rhythms. Everyone has his or her favorite type of music, but a dancer should appreciate the variety music can offer. Some tunes will make you move slowly, others faster. Some may make you feel like jumping around or even spinning. However the music inspires you, always have fun, because that is what music and dance are all about.

M is for the Music
that inspires you to make
new and exciting movements
with every step you take.

M
m

A holiday tradition in North America, the *Nutcracker* is possibly the most well-known ballet. Loved by audiences of all ages, it is also a wonderful introduction to dancing. This ballet is a Christmas tradition because the story is set at Christmastime and revolves around a very special gift of a nutcracker doll. Magic swirls through this story about children, incredible journeys, battles, royalty, and a beautiful fairy. Because the *Nutcracker*'s performances always feature children it is exciting for kids to watch as well as inspiring and motivating if they have any desire to dance.

N is for the *Nutcracker*
    where the story of Clara is told.
Her travels to magic kingdoms
        are loved by young and old.

With her prince by her side
    it may begin to seem
meeting the Sugarplum Fairy
            only happened in a dream.

N
n

Oo

Everyone dances differently and the exact same choreography will look a little different from one dancer to the next. It is these differences that make each dancer special. There are times when it is important to move the same as everyone else on the stage, but there are also times to enjoy one's own originality.

Dance has been blessed with many original artists who have contributed to its evolution. A good example is Isadora Duncan (1877–1927). In a time when ballet was highly regarded, she found it too rigid and unnatural. Rebelling against the strict rules of ballet, she developed a style that was much more natural and free. Inspired by the classics, especially the Greek myths, Isadora's dancing celebrated nature and the human form. Criticized by many in her time, she always stayed true to herself and her beliefs. Today she is celebrated, and her dancing is said to contain the roots of modern dance.

In a competitive art form, finding your individual style and not simply trying to copy somebody else can be a challenge. If you are able to truly focus and find what really drives you, and nurture that, you will shine from the inside.

O is for Original—
that is what you are!
Be true to yourself
and you will go far.

The pointe shoe made its first appearance in the 1800s. In the middle of the Romantic Era, with its love of all things spiritual and otherworldly, pointe shoes allowed the ballerina to give the illusion of floating across the stage. The term *en pointe* is often used to describe dancing *on* pointe shoes. Responsible for the development of the ballerina's technique, and replacing the traditional heeled dance shoe, the pointe shoe has become a critical aspect of ballet. Made out of satin, paper, and burlap (not wood, as many people think) today's pointe shoe looks very much the same today as it did in the 1800s. Ribbons, though often overlooked, are a very important part of the pointe shoe and play a crucial role. Not only are they beautiful to look at, they help the dancer get the most support out of her shoe. The ribbons usually match the color of the shoe, which also matches the tights, and this helps create a longer line. Generally the color of choice is pink or a light salmon but on occasion the satin is dyed to accommodate the look of a specific costume design.

P p

P is for Pointe shoes
with pretty pink bows.
Girls wear them while dancing
to stand on their toes.

When they work, dancers are always aware of the quality of their movement and especially the lines of their body. During the rehearsal period it is very helpful to use mirrors, which act as constant reminders to the dancers, so that they can make the corrections necessary to keep their quality of line intact.

When it comes to a jump, not only is the quality of the jump important, but so is the quality of the landing. Dancers strive for quiet landings in order to make them look effortless. Also, any steps performed *en pointe* should be as quiet as possible to preserve the illusion that the dancer floats on stage.

Another good quality in a dancer is the ability to learn new steps quickly. This is especially important when working with a choreographer on a new production. The choreographer creates brand-new steps, and relies on the dancers to be able to carry out his or her vision. The quicker the dancers are able to learn the steps and translate them to their bodies, the easier it is for the choreographer to create a ballet.

Qq

Q is for Quality, Quiet, and Quick.
These three words will do the trick.
They're good goals for when you dance
so give quality, quiet, and quick a chance.

R r

For all ballet students the highlight of the year is the moment they get to perform in front of their peers, friends, and family at their school's recital. It is the closest experience a young dancer can have to performing as a professional dancer!

The teacher will decide what the program will consist of and will make sure that every student dances the roles that best suit him or her in order to showcase the individual dancer's strengths. Schools take pride in these shows and a lot of dedication and attention to detail are put into them. Parents are usually asked to get involved in the creation of sets and costumes. The rehearsal period may last several months. It takes practice and repetition to learn the choreography. Eventually the practiced routine will make you feel like you own your own steps. It is only then that you can go on stage and perform. On your recital day everything comes together and that special magic is created on stage. It is the moment dancers live for.

R is for the Recital,
　　the goal of each rehearsal day.
Everyone will be there to see you
　　from near and far away.

　　You're ready in your costume.
　　　　You're waiting for your sign.
You've dreamed of this moment.
　　　　Now is your time to shine!

Stretching is a fundamental part of every dancer's training. By adding stretching to your dancing day at a young age, you will develop an important habit that will give you so many benefits as you grow. By stretching regularly, you will increase muscle flexibility, which is important when you want to create beautiful lines with your body. Stretching also helps reduce muscular soreness and tension, allowing your body to perform better. It will also help reduce the risk of injury and lengthens a dancer's career.

But stretching should not be done only by dancers or just during dance class. Everyone can benefit by making stretching a daily routine. Just remember that stretching is most beneficial when muscles are warm, so do not rush into it and try a light warm-up before you stretch.

S is for Stretching—
    something you must do
before you start your day
    and when you end it, too.

T t

T is for the Theater
where the stage will transform
and create a world of magic
as the dancers perform.

The theater is often thought of as the dancer's home, and the stage his or her favorite place to be. During a performing season, a professional dancer will spend six days a week in the theater.

The process of rehearsing for a new production is a gratifying one, but nothing compares to the feeling of standing onstage in front of an audience. The music, scenery, lighting, costumes, and dance all come together to create the magic that transports the performers and the audience to a different world. It takes many people to create this magic. The dancers and musicians are the ones that everyone sees, but behind the scenes are many active participants that the audience is not aware of.

Stage managers are in charge of people called stagehands, who make sure lighting cues and changes of scenery happen on time. A wardrobe department also works in the wings, making sure that costumes look good, and helping with quick costume changes. The wig department is also busy and on call during the show, helping with any hair changes needed. All of the people involved make up a big family that works together to give the audience an experience they will never forget.

U u

U is for the Universal language
that in ballet you must choose.
To identify every step
it is French that you must use.

U is for the Universal language
that in ballet you must choose.
To identify every step
it is French that you must use.

Have you ever wondered why all the terminology in ballet is in French? The person responsible for that is King Louis XIV of France, who established the first professional ballet academy. This was the first time that a group of ballet teachers worked together under one roof to create a system to teach professional dancers. Positions and steps were given names and recorded. Because this occurred in France, the language of choice was French. The French names established by the earliest dance schools are the same names that we use today to identify ballet steps and movements. If you translate them to English you will realize that they were not randomly chosen. In fact, most of the French words describe the action of the step.

For example:
Tendu—pointed foot with leg stretched out straight
Frappé—a quick striking movement of the leg
Batterie—steps to which beats are added
Rond de jambe en l'air—circle of the leg in the air
Plié—bending of the knee or knees
Pas de cheval—a horse step

Agrippina Vaganova (1879–1951) retired in 1916 from the Imperial Russian Ballet to pursue a career in teaching dance. Even though as a dancer she attained the title of prima ballerina, she is better known for being the founder of the Vaganova school and method, also known as the Russian method. This method focuses on training the body as a harmony, giving special attention to the placement of the back and arms as well as developing the flexibility and the endurance of the dancer. Considered one of the most well-known methods of teaching, today it is used all over the world.

Just as with Vaganova, most well-known methods carry their founder's name. The Cecchetti or Italian method is named after Enrico Cecchetti; the Bournonville or Danish method is named after August Bournonville; and the Balanchine method used by the New York City Ballet is named after George Balanchine.

V
v

V is for Vaganova;
        Agrippina was her name.
Despite her great dancing,
        it would not bring her fame.

She created a new method
        so complete and so great
that it is used around the world.
        To be a teacher was her fate.

If you are thinking of becoming a dancer, be prepared to love warm-ups. All dancers need to start their day with a good warm-up in order to prepare the body for the very high physical demands ahead of them. Floor exercises that target specific muscle groups, light stretching, and warm clothing are all part of a good warm-up. Backs, hips, and ankles are body parts that dancers will give special attention to, and so it is common to see them wearing back braces, an extra layer of shorts, and leg warmers before and between rehearsals. These items are usually knits made of wool or cotton and are designed to offer the dancer a full range of movement while keeping his or her muscles warm.

The body of a dancer is a finely tuned instrument that requires good maintenance in order to perform at its best. That is why the warm-up is an essential part of a dancer's daily routine.

W is for Warm-up,
    with small moves and warm clothes.
  It gets your body ready
      from your head to your toes.

X x

If you ever get the chance to step on a stage before a dance performance, you will notice several pieces of tape on the floor. These are markings that help the dancers know where they should be on the stage in order to make the choreography fit with the whole company of dancers and the set.

The first marking is placed at center stage. Located in the very middle, it is the most important marking because all the other markings are made in relation to this point. Markings that divide the stage into quarters and eighths are also placed at the front of the stage for the dancers' use. Stage managers lay down markings of their own that let them know where certain pieces of scenery and props should be placed.

X marks the center stage
that shows the dancers how
to keep their pirouettes centered
and where to take their bow.

Today the tutu is the most recognizable costume that a ballerina wears. There are three different styles depending on the style of the dance. The romantic tutu exposes ankles and feet and is very soft and airy. The bell tutu has a similar look but its skirt is knee length. The classical tutu has an even shorter skirt and is flat-shaped, like a pancake. It is the iconic image of a girl in a tutu that has inspired so many to dream of becoming a ballerina.

The spotlight is the lighting most craved by a dancer onstage. It singles out the main characters, allowing the audience to recognize them throughout the performance. Lighting is essential, because without lighting the experience of the performance would not be complete. Romeo and Juliet's balcony pas de deux would not have the same intimate feel without moonlight shining on them, nor would *Swan Lake* have the same haunting feeling if the lighting were removed.

Lighting designers work closely with the choreographers and set designers to develop a look and create the right mood for each scene. Overhead lights, side lighting, and spotlights are combined to create many effects from night to day, from dawns to sunsets, and for silhouettes or pools of light on an otherwise dark stage.

Y y

Y is for the Yellow tutu you adore,
          or the yellow star upon your door.
And the audience cheers when you are through
          as a yellow spotlight shines right on you.

Zippers are helpful in ballet costumes when dancers have a quick costume change during a performance. In most cases, when a quick change is not needed, rows of hooks are used so that the costume size can be changed.

In the early days of ballet, costumes reflected the richness and perfection of the French courts, but these costumes were cumbersome and allowed for very little movement. Men wore elaborate trousers and heavy coats and often had swords attached to their waist. Women wore tight corsets with long heavy skirts and long sleeves. In time the costumes changed, allowing for more intricate dance steps and movements. Today men are usually seen in tights made of Lycra and short jackets with tails. For women, skirts were shortened to highlight the leg and footwork and to facilitate spins.

Z z

Z is for the Zip of the Zipper.
And now the dancer is prepared
to play the role of the evil wizard
and make everybody scared.

A pointed hat, a long cape,
and a wand for the fight—
each dancer always needs
his costume to be just right.